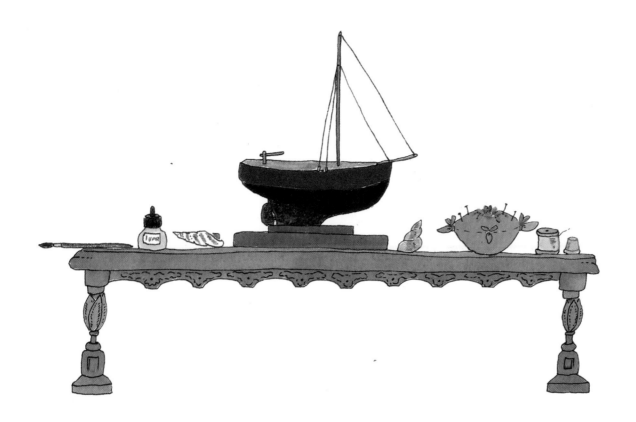

Louise Builds a Boat

LOUISE PFANNER

ORCHARD BOOKS   NEW YORK

For Tim

You can read the flags from left to right.
The key is on the endpapers. Look for messages
on Louise's boat throughout the book.

I am going to build a boat.

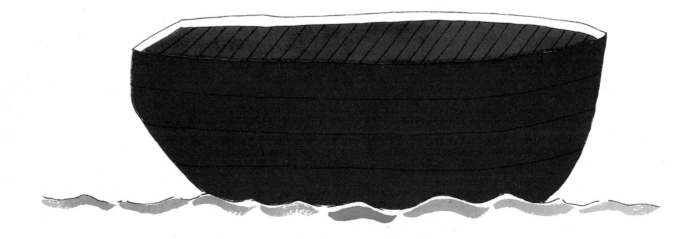

with a wooden deck

to play games on,

and a mast

for the boatswain's chair.

I will make a crow's nest

so I can watch the dolphins play,

and signal flags

to dress the boat.

There will be a gangplank

for diving practice,

and a figurehead

to paint on.

I will build a cabin

to sleep in,

and a galley

to cook in.

There must be an anchor

to hold me safe in a storm,

and lanterns

to light the night sky.

I will have a dinghy

to carry provisions,

and canvas sails

to catch the wind.

When the boat is finished

I shall call her...

and then I'll sail around the world

to visit all my friends.

First published in Australia by John Ferguson Pty Ltd.

Orchard Books, A division of Franklin Watts, Inc.
387 Park Avenue South, New York, NY 10016

Manufactured in the United States of America. Printed by General Offset Co., Inc.
Bound by Horowitz/Rae. Book design by Mina Greenstein. The text of this book is set in
20 pt. ITC Novarese Medium. The illustrations are pen and ink and watercolors,
reproduced in full color. 10 9 8 7 6 5 4 3 2 1

Library of Congress Cataloging-in-Publication Data
Pfanner, Louise. Louise builds a boat / Louise Pfanner. p. cm. Summary: Louise
imagines building her ideal boat, one with a wooden deck for games, a crow's nest for
watching dolphins, and a figurehead to paint.
ISBN 0-531-05888-3. ISBN 0-531-08488-4 (lib. bdg.)
[1. Boats and boating—Fiction.] I. Title. PZ7.P44853Ln 1990 [E]—dc20
89-70929 CIP AC

N

Q

O

R

P

T

Y

V

X

S

U

Z

W